This book belongs to

_____

A Crown for Atta

Published by Advance Publishers
www.advance-publishers.com

Written by Catherine McCafferty
Illustrated by Chris Bolden, Ken Becker, and Brian Sebern
Editorial development and management by Bumpy Slide Books
Illustrations produced by Disney Publishing Creative Development
Cover design by Deborah Boone

ISBN: 1-57973-020-5

Atta held onto her crown as she ran toward the anthill. She had so much to do now that she was a queen! She had just met with Cornelius about the harvest. Now she had to meet with her mother and the others about the harvest festival.

"Atta! Hey, Atta! Over here!" Flik called to her as she rushed by.

Not wanting to hurt Flik's feelings, Atta stopped and waited.

"Look what I made for the harvest festival," Flik said. He stood next to a strange-looking device. "Wait till you see this work!"

Atta smiled. Flik was always building new things. "What is it?" she asked.

"Just stand right there!" Flik replied. "Wow! You're really going to like this! See, there's this air pump over here. And it sends air in through this tube. And then—"

"Er, Flik, I'm in a little bit of a hurry," Atta said.

"Oh. Right. I'll just show you what it does."

Flik put his foot down on the air tube. *Poof!* Flower petals flew into the air. "I call it a Petal Poofer," he said proudly. "It will be our entertainment for the harvest festival."

"That's great, Flik!" Atta said as she set off toward the anthill.

"Wait!" said Flik. "If you look inside . . ."

Atta turned and stepped closer. Her foot came down on the air tube. *Poof!* Flik flew into the air. So did Atta's crown!

"Flik, are you all right?" Atta cried.

Flik looked more happy than hurt. "Hey! That'll make a great ride for the Blueberries!" he said.

Relieved, Atta reached up to straighten her crown. That's when she noticed it wasn't there!

"I'll help you find it!" Flik offered. "I'm sure it's close by. None of the petals ever poofs very far."

"It's not a petal, Flik. It's a crown!" exclaimed Atta as she searched the ground.

"What is everyone going to think about a new queen who can't even hold onto her crown?" Atta cried.

"Not to worry. I'll find it," declared Flik. "I'll just build a crown detector and—"

"Flik, the crown got lost because of your Petal Poofer," explained Atta. "Don't build something new to make it worse!" She sighed. "I'm late for my meeting! I have to go. I don't know what I'm going to tell them about the crown."

Flik ran ahead of Atta. Picking up strips of grass, he quickly wove them into a crown.

"Here, Atta," said Flik, "wear this instead."

Atta jammed the crown on her head. "It's not the same, Flik," she said angrily. "Please, just find the real crown."

19

The meeting had already started by the time Atta
arrived. Everyone looked up as she entered.

"What's that you're wearing?" asked her mother.

"Um, my everyday crown," said Atta. "I'm wearing

it so nothing will happen to the real one,"
she explained, thinking quickly.

Her mother beamed. "What a good idea!"

The others murmured their agreement.

"Now then," said Thorny, "when should we have the harvest party?"

Atta was too worried about her crown to decide. "Let's talk about that later," she said.

"Should my students make invitations?" asked Mr. Soil.

"Let's decide that later, too," replied Atta.

Atta's mother looked over at her daughter. She could see that Atta was worried about something.

"Why don't we just have this meeting some other time?" Atta's mother suggested.

"I think that's a good idea," said Atta.

As the others left, Atta's mother turned to her. "Is something wrong, dear?"

"I'm just no good at being a queen," Atta said.

"Well, you just started, dear. It's a bit soon to decide that," her mother told her.

"But look what I've done already," said Atta. "I've yelled at Flik. I can't decide anything about this harvest party. And I've . . . I've lost my crown."

"You lost your crown?" her mother repeated. "I thought you said—"

"I didn't want the others to know," Atta said, taking off the grass crown. "They wouldn't listen to me if they thought I couldn't even take care of my crown."

"Atta," her mother said, "your crown is not as important as how you treat the other ants."

"I'd feel better if I told Flik I was sorry," said Atta.

"Well, Atta," said her mother, "you're a better queen than you think. Because now you know that the ants in this colony are more important than any crown."

Atta hurried out and found Flik's Petal Poofer right where he had left it. But the air pump and part of the tube were gone.

Atta figured Flik must be out searching for her crown. She knew she would need help finding him.

Atta ran to get some of the Blueberries. She took a deep breath and said, "Flik is gone, and so is my crown. We need to find Flik first."

The ants split into two groups and began their search.

Dot led her group over to the wheat field. Flik was not there. Then they looked over leaves and under tree roots nearby. Dot even climbed to the top of a dandelion. But there was no sign of Flik.

"All right, Blueberries," said Dot, "let's check the swamp."

The Blueberries shivered with fear, but they had to find Flik.

Atta and another Blueberry started their search at the Petal Poofer. They followed the trail of flower petals until it ended among some grass stalks. When Atta got closer, she saw a strange device in the grass.

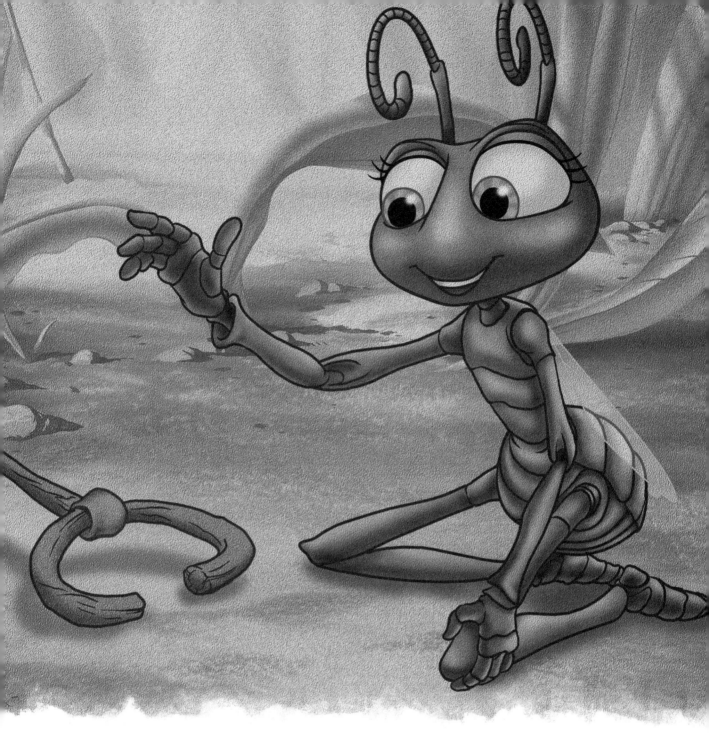

"The crown detector!" cried Atta. So Flik had built
it anyway! Atta had to smile.

"Flik!" she called out, hoping he might be nearby.

Atta heard someone calling her, but it was not Flik.

"Atta!" Dot cried. She came charging over. "Follow us! We found something!"

At the edge of the swamp, Dot pointed to the
air pump and the tube from Flik's Petal Poofer.

"Oh, no!" exclaimed Atta. "Flik must have fallen
into the swamp!"

Atta was just about to send the Blueberries for help when the swamp water began to ripple. The end of the tube poked above the water. Then Flik's head popped up, too!

"How do you like my underwater search suit?" Flik asked.

Atta was so happy to see him that she gave him a hug.

"Atta, I'm sorry about your crown," said Flik.

Atta shook her head. "No, I'm sorry, Flik. I'm sorry I yelled at you. Besides, I can always wear the grass one."

"But you don't have to," Flik said. "I found the real crown!" He bowed and held it out to Atta. Atta gratefully took the crown. "Come on, everybody," she said. "We've got a party to plan!"

The next day at the harvest party, Atta was surrounded by her family and friends. She felt lucky, indeed. In fact, she felt just like a queen!

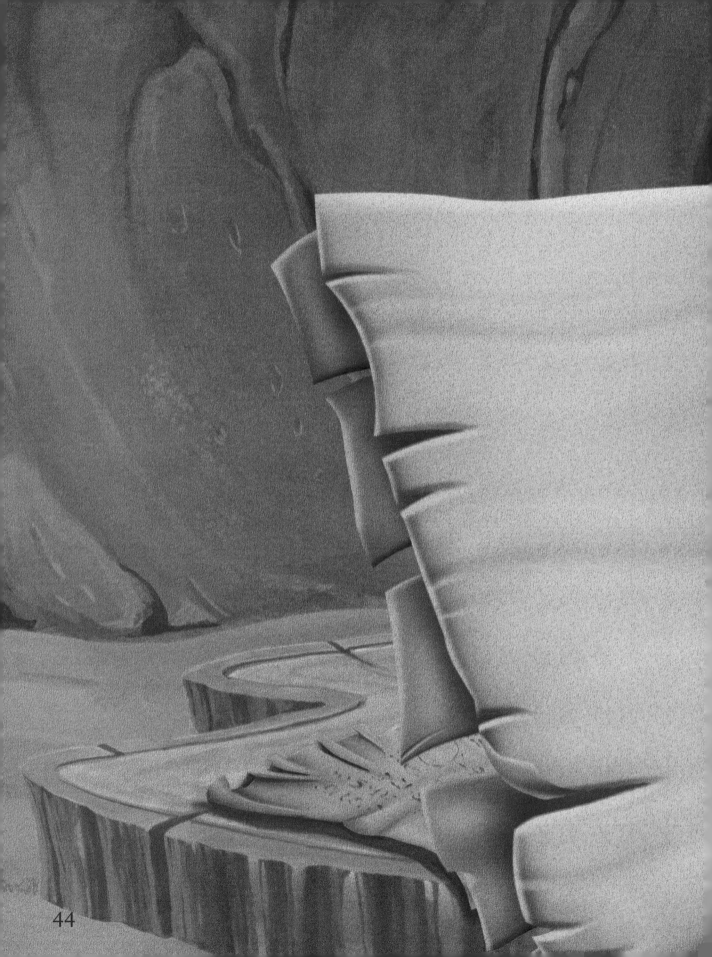

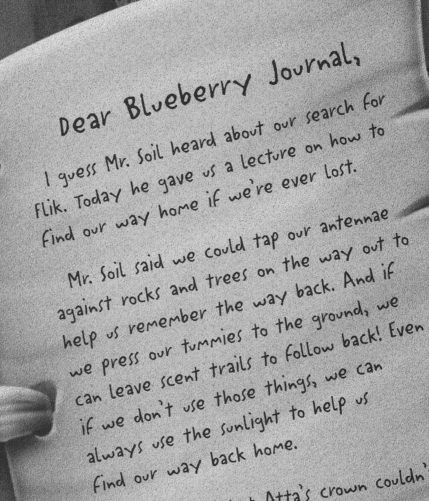

Dear Blueberry Journal,

I guess Mr. Soil heard about our search for Flik. Today he gave us a lecture on how to find our way home if we're ever lost.

Mr. Soil said we could tap our antennae against rocks and trees on the way out to help us remember the way back. And if we press our tummies to the ground, we can leave scent trails to follow back! Even if we don't use those things, we can always use the sunlight to help us find our way back home.

It's too bad that Atta's crown couldn't find its way home. That would have saved us a lot of time!

Till next time,
Dot